Put Beginning Readers on the Right Track with
ALL ABOARD READING™

The All Aboard Reading series is especially for beginning readers. Written by noted authors and illustrated in full color, these are books that children really and truly *want* to read—books to excite their imagination, tickle their funny bone, expand their interests, and support their feelings. With four different reading levels, All Aboard Reading lets you choose which books are most appropriate for your children and their growing abilities.

Picture Readers—for Ages 3 to 6
Picture Readers have super-simple texts, with many nouns appearing as rebus pictures. At the end of each book are 24 flash cards—on one side is the rebus picture; on the other side is the written-out word.

Level 1—for Preschool through First-Grade Children
Level 1 books have very few lines per page, very large type, easy words, lots of repetition, and pictures with visual "cues" to help children figure out the words on the page.

Level 2—for First-Grade to Third-Grade Children
Level 2 books are printed in slightly smaller type than Level 1 books. The stories are more complex, but there is still lots of repetition in the text, and many pictures. The sentences are quite simple and are broken up into short lines to make reading easier.

Level 3—for Second-Grade through Third-Grade Children
Level 3 books have considerably longer texts, harder words, and more complicated sentences.

All Aboard for happy reading!

For Darío—J.D.

For Mom and Dad—Thanks for your love and
support throughout the years. Love, D.O.

Text copyright © 2000 by Jennifer Dussling. Illustrations copyright © 2000 by Denise
Ortakales. All rights reserved. Published by Grosset & Dunlap, a division of Penguin Putnam
Books for Young Readers, New York. ALL ABOARD READING is a trademark of Penguin
Putnam Inc. GROSSET & DUNLAP is a trademark of Penguin Putnam Inc. Published
simultaneously in Canada. Printed in the U.S.A

Library of Congress Cataloging-in-Publication Data

Dussling, Jennifer
    Planets / by Jennifer Dussling ; illustrated by Denise Ortakales.
        p. cm. -- (All aboard reading. Level 2)
    ISBN 0-448-42406-1 (pbk.) -- ISBN 0-448-42416-9 (gb)
        1. Planets--Juvenile literature. I. Ortakales, Denise, ill. II. Title. III. Series.

QB602 .D87 2000
    523.4--dc21   00-059601

ISBN 0-448-42416-9 (GB)   A B C D E F G H I J
ISBN 0-448-42406-1 (pbk)   A B C D E F G H I J

ALL
ABOARD
READING™

Level 2
Grades 1-3

PLANETS

By Jennifer Dussling
Illustrated by Denise Ortakales

Grosset & Dunlap • New York

Long ago, in Greece,

people looked at the night sky.

They saw the moon.

They saw bright stars.

They also saw other objects

that moved across the sky.

They called them <u>planetes</u>.

In Greek that means wanderer.

That's where we get the word "planet."

We live on the planet called Earth.

Earth circles the sun.

So do eight other planets.

Mars

Mercury

Earth

Venus

Sun

asteroid
belt

Uranus

Pluto

Jupiter

Neptune

Saturn

The sun and the nine planets
are called the solar system.

For a long time people thought that
the sun circled Earth!
One man said that was wrong.
His name was Copernicus.
(You say it like this—coe-purr-nuh-kuss.)
In 1513, he had a new idea.
He said that Earth circled the sun.

He wrote a book about it.

The book did not come out

until thirty years later!

Most people thought that

his idea was crazy.

But Copernicus was right.

The sun is the center

of the solar system.

Each planet has its own path

around the sun.

The paths are not really circles.

They are more like ovals.

The paths are called orbits.

The time it takes for a planet
to travel around the sun is a year.
An Earth year is 365 days.
Planets also spin.
A day is the time it takes for a planet
to make a complete spin.
On Earth a day is
twenty-four hours long.

Mercury is the closest planet
to the sun.

It circles the sun in eighty-eight days.

So on Mercury,
a year is only eighty-eight days long.

How old are you in Mercury years?

Mercury is a small planet
with craters and cliffs.

It has no moons.

Mercury gets very hot during the day
and very cold at night.

The next planet is Venus.

You can see it

in the morning sky.

It looks white and beautiful.

Long ago,

Romans named

the planets after their gods.

We still use the Roman names.

Mercury was the messenger
of the gods.

Venus was
the goddess of beauty.

Mars was the god
of war.

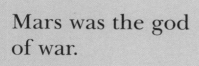

Venus is the hottest planet.

The temperature on Venus is 900° F!

That is much hotter than an oven.

Why is Venus hotter than Mercury?

After all, Mercury is closer to the sun.

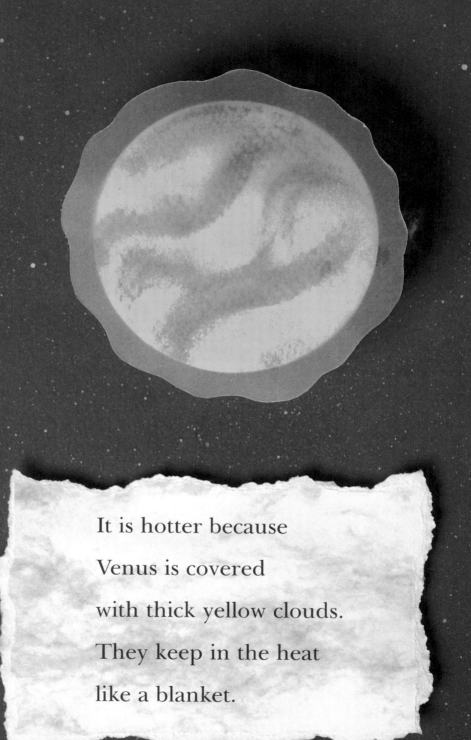

It is hotter because
Venus is covered
with thick yellow clouds.
They keep in the heat
like a blanket.

Earth is the third planet from the sun.
Earth is the only planet with life on it—
people, animals, and plants.
It is in the perfect place,
not too close to the sun
and not too far away.
On Earth we have plenty of water.
Without water there can be no life.
Earth also has a thin layer
of gases around it.
This is the air we breathe.
These gases also block out
harmful light from the sun.

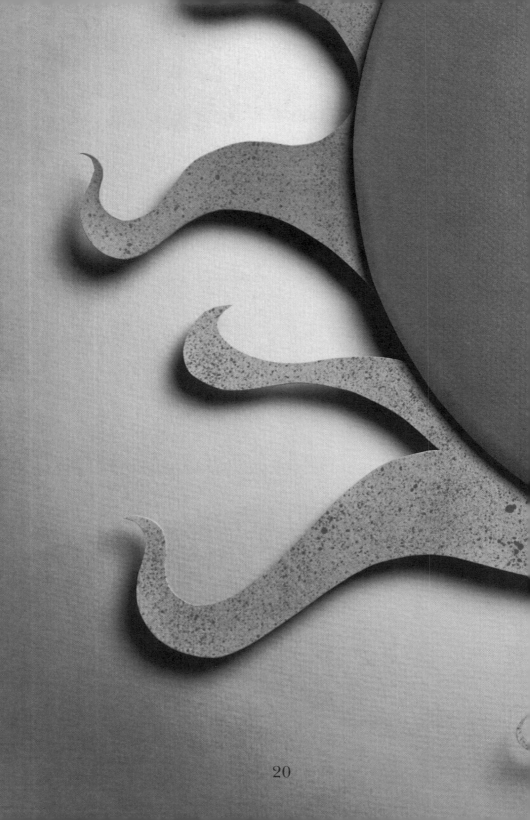

The planet after Earth is Mars.

Mars has dusty red soil.

The red dust in the air

makes the sky look pink.

Sometimes Mars has dust storms

that last for months.

Can you guess why the red planet

was named after the war god?

It is because red is the color of blood.

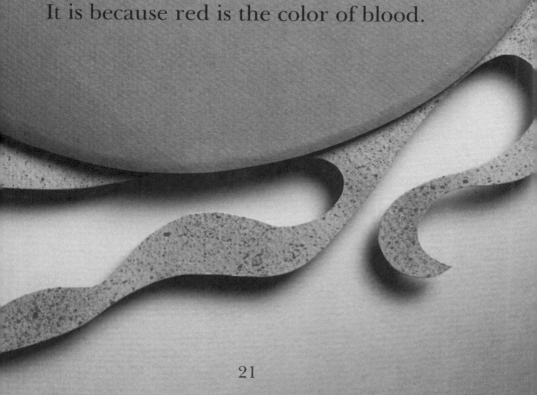

There are a lot of stories about little green men from Mars. They are not true.

True

Not True

22

But at one time,

maybe there was some kind of life on Mars.

In 1996, a little rock made big news.

Scientists found the rock in Antarctica.

Long ago it had fallen from Mars.

The rock had a fossil in it,

a fossil of tiny cells.

Because of this,

some scientists think that

there may have been

some kind of life on Mars.

Mars also has ice caps

and channels that

may have carried water.

Why is that so important?

Because all living things need water.

So some scientists think that
maybe people could live on Mars.
Maybe some day far in the future,
we will build a city there!

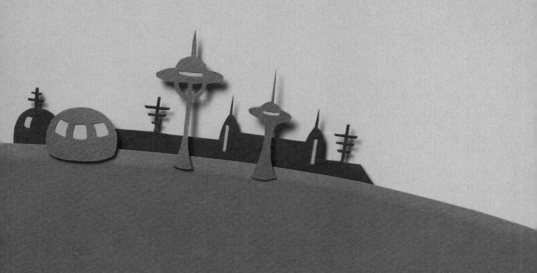

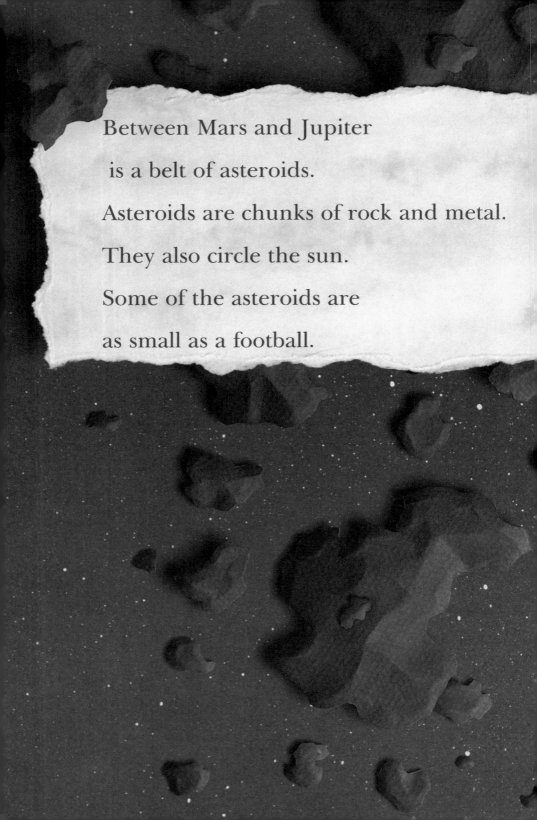

Between Mars and Jupiter
is a belt of asteroids.
Asteroids are chunks of rock and metal.
They also circle the sun.
Some of the asteroids are
as small as a football.

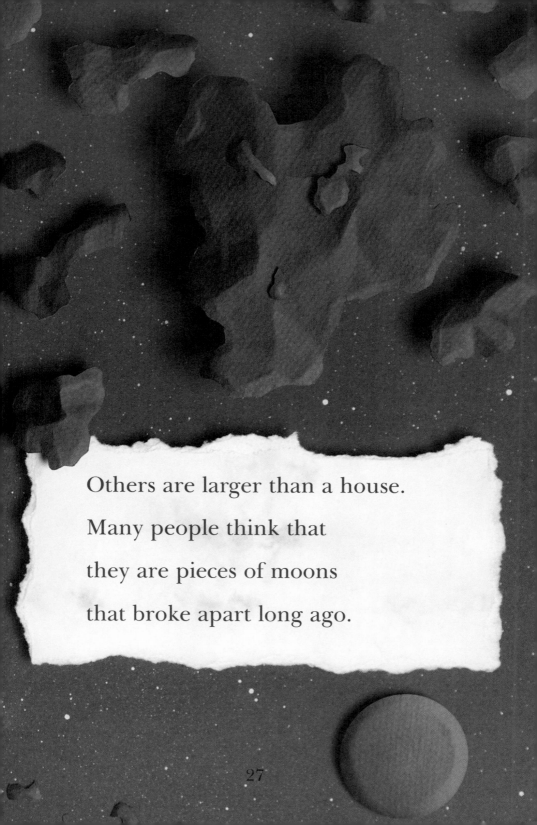

Others are larger than a house.

Many people think that

they are pieces of moons

that broke apart long ago.

Jupiter is the fifth planet from the sun.

Jupiter is huge!

It is the largest planet in the solar system.

It is much larger than Earth.

Think of Jupiter and Earth like this:

If Earth were the size of a pea,

Jupiter would be the size of an orange.

Jupiter doesn't look at all like
Mercury, Venus, Earth, or Mars.
Jupiter is made mostly of gas, not rock.
So are the next three planets—
Saturn, Uranus, and Neptune.

Saturn

Uranus

Neptune

Jupiter

Jupiter is a stormy place.

See the red circle on Jupiter?

That is called the Great Red Spot.

It is like a super hurricane.

Strong winds blow.

Lightning bolts crack

through the clouds.

This storm has been raging

for hundreds of years!

Earth is not the only planet with a moon.

Jupiter has at least sixteen!

How is a moon different from a planet?

A moon orbits a planet.

It does not orbit the sun.

Beyond Jupiter is Saturn.
In 1610, a man named Galileo
first looked at Saturn
through a telescope.

He was very surprised.

There was a bump

on either side of the planet.

Saturn had ears!

Can you guess what Galileo saw?

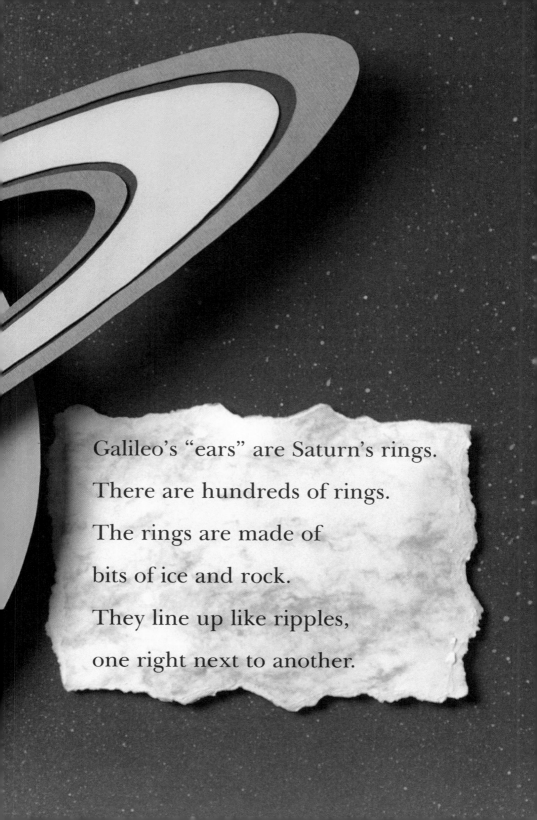

Galileo's "ears" are Saturn's rings.

There are hundreds of rings.

The rings are made of

bits of ice and rock.

They line up like ripples,

one right next to another.

For hundreds of years
people thought that
Saturn was the only planet
with rings around it.
But it's not.
Uranus, the seventh planet,
does too.
Its rings are made
of chunks of black rocks.
Uranus is a tippy planet.
It lies on its side.

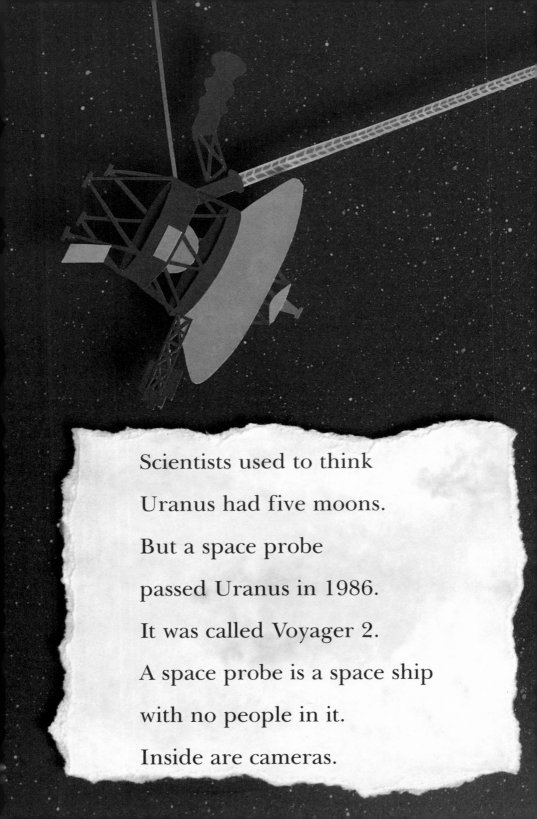

Scientists used to think
Uranus had five moons.
But a space probe
passed Uranus in 1986.
It was called Voyager 2.
A space probe is a space ship
with no people in it.
Inside are cameras.

The cameras on Voyager 2
took lots of pictures
and sent them to Earth.
The pictures showed
many more moons
near Uranus.
They also showed that
Uranus had rings.

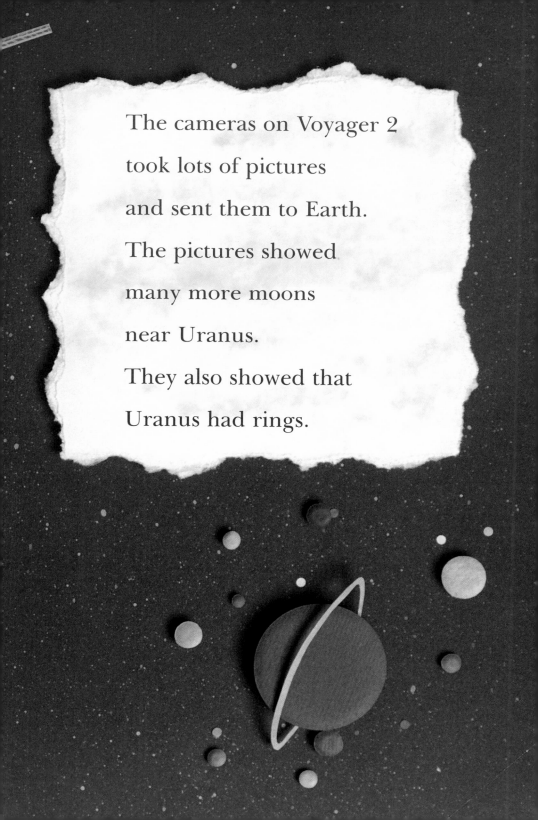

Neptune was the god of the sea.

He could whip up storms

on the water.

So Neptune is a good name

for the next planet.

It is blue–green

and it has the fastest winds

on any planet.

They can reach 700 miles an hour.

Neptune sometimes has a spot—

the Great Dark Spot.

It is another huge storm.

The planet Pluto was not
found until 1930.
It is a small planet.
It is very cold.
That is because it is so far
from the sun.
It takes Pluto 248 years
to travel once
around the sun.

Pluto

Neptune

Pluto has a very strange orbit.
For twenty years out of the 248,
Pluto travels inside Neptune's orbit.
During that time,
Neptune becomes the farthest planet
from the sun.

it so small

has a crazy orbit,

me scientists think that

Pluto was once a moon of Neptune.

But somehow it went into its own orbit.

So, is Pluto really a planet?

Some scientists don't think so.

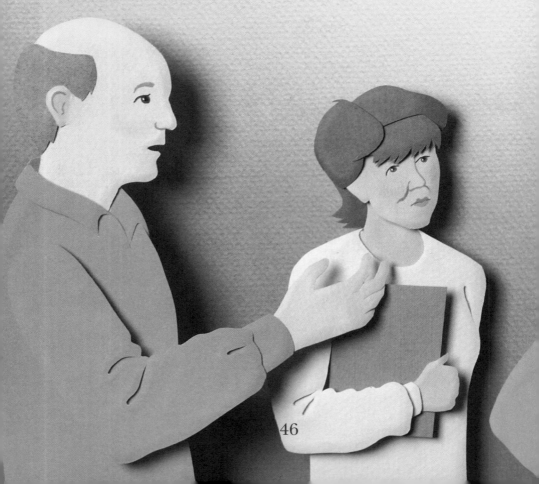

They want to drop Pluto

from the list of planets.

Then the solar system

will have only eight planets.

But other scientists think that

Pluto is a planet.

For now, Pluto is still listed as a planet.

What is out there past Pluto?

Lots and lots of stars.

Lots of other solar systems.

We've sent probes past Pluto.

They are headed to the faraway stars.

Who knows what they will find!